# "What are you doing today, Henry?"

Cataloging in Publication Data appears on last page.

123456789 RABP 7898765

# "What are you doing today, Henry?"

BY LOUANNE NORRIS          ILLUSTRATED BY LARRY ROSS

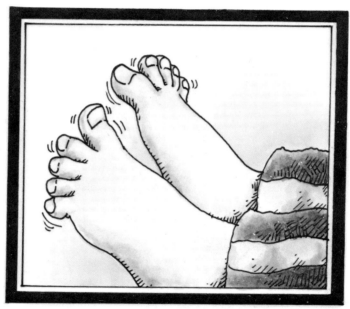

## McGRAW-HILL BOOK COMPANY

New York  St. Louis  San Francisco  Düsseldorf  Johannesburg  Kuala Lumpur  London  Mexico
Montreal  New Delhi  Panama  Paris  São Paulo  Singapore  Sydney  Tokyo  Toronto

When he opened his eyes Henry saw that his blue animal poster and his red star and planet poster were staring at him. It was very quiet. His brother Daniel must be up. Just to check, Henry pulled himself over to the edge of the mattress and looked down on a pile of rumpled sheets.

He wiggled his toes. Now he could really enjoy himself. He could even hear noises from the street four floors below—footsteps and words.

But then, Daniel poked his head into the room. "What's the matter? You still lying around?"

Henry pretended to be asleep. Nothing perfect lasts, Henry thought. Of all the people in the world, why did he have to share a bedroom with Daniel on the fourth floor of an apartment building in the middle of the city?

Daniel kept right on going: "Breakfast," he warned and slammed the door.

Henry slid down the worn bedpost at the end of the bunkbed. He slid into his summer shorts, his sneakers, and he slid down the hall.

And he slid into his seat at the table and put his sneakered feet on his table leg. Just like he always did.

His father said, "Well, what are you doing today, Henry?"

He could tell—no one was going to the beach or the store. No one had any time for him. Everyone had plans. He could feel how busy everyone was. Daniel, with his baseball cap, was going out for practice.

He'd better not say anything. He couldn't say
"There's nothing to do," or "I haven't decided," or
"I don't know yet," or "I don't have to have any plans."
His mother would think of some useful thing to do,
or maybe a whole lot of things he might like to do—
some other day. "Why don't you…" he could hear
her say.

It was a puzzle. He was on his own but he better
not let anyone know.

"I…" said Henry.

"You…" said Daniel.

"Daniel," said his mother to Daniel. And then
to Henry, "Be sure to be home for lunch, dear." And
then "Pass the toast, please," giving everyone a
quick smile.

Henry was happy his mother was too busy to notice he hadn't even answered her. He scooped up the toast plate. It knocked over the sugarbowl. Sugar spurted out over the tabletop. Everyone else rushed around in a big hurry. Doing the right thing, Henry thought. His mother mopped up grains of sugar and pushed around toast crumbs. Daniel glared. His father just gathered up the newspaper.

All of a sudden that was the end of breakfast. And all of a sudden he was outside, under the apartment house awning, looking up and down the street for something he might want to do.

Joe at the newsstand called him over. "Hey
Henry, give me a hand."

Henry hoisted himself up on a stool behind the
newsstand and wrapped his sneakered feet around
the stool legs. Joe was busy handing out newspapers
and picking up dimes, nickels, and quarters that
tinkled on the countertop. Sometimes that was
Henry's job. Henry liked sliding them into the right
slots in a wooden tray—slots for nickels, quarters,
dimes, and pennies.

Henry noticed people lining up for papers, and
lining up at the bus stop, and disappearing down the
subway steps. "No, not today; sorry Joe," he said,
and he unwound his feet and slipped down off the
stool.

"What's up?" someone shouted in his ear. It was his best friend Tim. But Tim ran on without waiting and disappeared down the street into a crowd. For a minute Henry was ready to run off down the street with Tim to wherever Tim was going, or on whatever errand Tim was running, or even to do whatever Tim was doing. But he didn't.

The sidewalk was filled with people—people with shopping carts, people carrying newspapers, people holding hands. Even babies bounced by in carriages up, down, up, down.

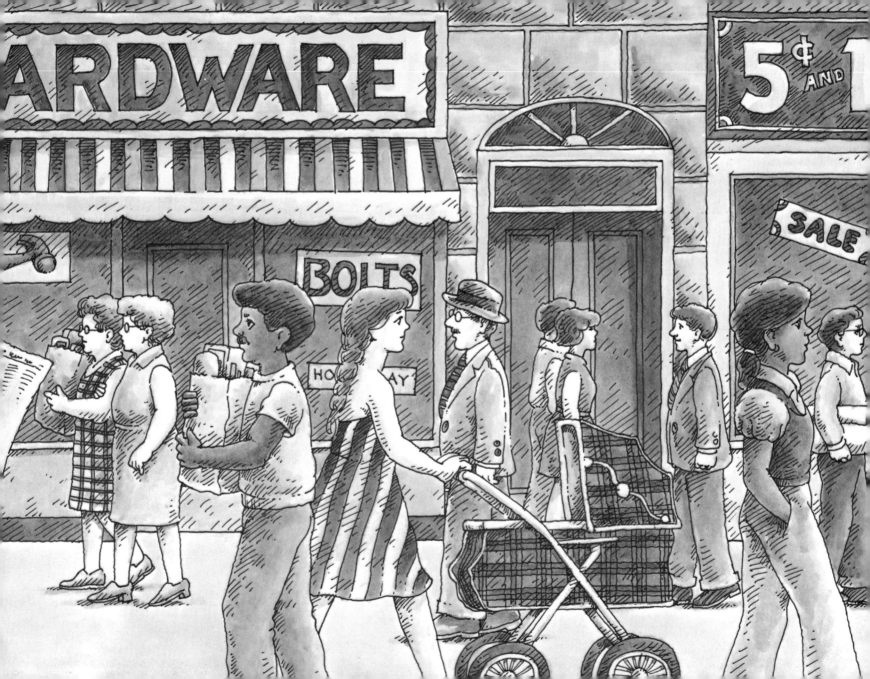

There was lots of noise in the street. Trucks rolled up to the curb delivering. Henry usually liked to watch them unloading food. He liked to watch cartons and crates and boxes with celery leaves poking out appear from the truck, lifted from hand to hand, and then come flying down by ramps into the dark bottom of the supermarket basement. But not today. He stepped out of the way of a carton of bluefish as it came sailing by.

He passed the schoolyard where Daniel and his friends practiced. Sometimes they'd let him field, but Henry didn't want to wait around today. Today, especially, he didn't want to look as if he wanted to play.

So he ran by the schoolyard and slowed down
for a couple of blocks and then he stopped next door
to his own apartment building. There, parked under
a NO PARKING sign, was an enormous station
wagon. On its front windshield in bold lettering was
a sign: MOVING. On its sides were painted waves
and a swimming fish and "Sammy's Fish Market"
in letters almost faded away. It was a beautiful wagon.

But it wasn't the station wagon that Henry stared at so much as the girl standing beside it. She reached into the station wagon and brought out a birdcage. She set it carefully on the sidewalk and started to talk to the bird inside. She opened the door of the birdcage. The black bird, who was so very black it was purple and green too, slowly lifted a long leg over the wires and stepped onto the sidewalk. The bird walked around in a circle, then flew around a tree, and back to the girl.

"Cocoa always comes back to me," the girl said to herself.

Just then a lady carrying packages and holding three dogs on leashes bumped into Henry. Henry lost his balance. He teetered, fell, then hit the sidewalk.

"What do you think you're doing, standing in the middle of the sidewalk?" screeched the lady, crossly. The old raincoat she was wearing flapped around her thin body. The dogs kept running around in circles and sniffing him and soon the leashes were wound around him. Now she was really angry. The dogs kept jumping on him and licking his face. The lady had to set her packages down, bend down, and untie Henry.

"This isn't funny at all," she said as she dragged her dogs down the street. They didn't want to go. They wanted to give Henry some more licks.

Henry didn't think it was funny either because now he was picked up by a strange man with bulging muscles, just as if he were going to dust him off. He felt helpless. I should have stayed in bed, he thought. And then he was furious. The girl who owned Cocoa was laughing.

He was furious while the man said, "That's life, kid."

And Henry was furious as he said, "I'm OK, I'm OK," to all the upturned faces looking at him.

"Let me down!" he cried as he saw his feet dangling in the air. He kicked wildly near the green waves painted on the side of the car. It was embarrassing. This was not what he wanted to be doing today.

"I'm Henry, from next door," he said as soon as he was put down. He felt better on his own two feet, more like himself again.

As if to prove something, Henry pointed to a paper bag, one of those set out on the sidewalk with other bags and boxes and cartons and lamps to be carried upstairs. And then Henry made a fist to show how strong he was.

"That's a lot of muscle, kid," said the man. Even Henry was surprised. And he felt proud.

So this was what he wanted to do today. The man with bulging muscles felt Henry's arm, just to check out whether Henry was really strong enough. "OK, kid." He smiled. Henry smiled back and hoisted a heavy box.

Up and downstairs went Henry, happy, even if
his muscles did ache. He wasn't used to climbing up
and down, up and down. He always took the elevator.

Luckily Daniel wasn't home for lunch at the same
time he was. As Henry swallowed the last of his
sandwich and milk, he mumbled "I'll be next door"
to his mother, and closed the apartment door behind
him.

By the time he got home that evening, Henry was very tired. He slipped into his seat at supper and parked his feet on the table leg. Henry couldn't wait for his father to ask him, "What happened today?"

Finally his father nodded at Henry, "What did you do today, Henry?"

"Well, I carried paper bags and boxes upstairs for some people next door," said Henry.

"Oh, did you have a job? How did that happen? You didn't tell us about that this morning," said his mother.

"No, it wasn't anything like a job. It happened more like an accident," Henry said.

"An accident!" yelled Daniel. "Oh, that kind of a day—that's pretty rotten."

"What kind of a day is that?" asked Henry. He really wanted to know. "I accidentally met this family."

"That's not an accident," said Daniel.

"Well, it was for me," Henry insisted. "I got tangled up with some dogs."

"Maybe you had an adventure," Henry's mother suggested.

He heard his father mumble "…valuable experience…" to his mother.

"I let the bird out of the cage…" interrupted Henry.

"Another accident!" said Daniel.

"That's what I thought, but nobody cared. Cocoa flew all around before she flew back to her owner. She knows where she is."

Disgusted, Daniel said, "Nothing that makes sense to you makes sense to me. All I know is you wouldn't play ball, so what did you do?"

"That's all you know! All you know about is how to play ball." Henry was angry.

"Henry…Daniel…Daniel…Henry," said their mother.

"That's enough boys," said Henry's father. His mother and father said they were glad he had been so helpful and what was the name of the new neighbors? Henry had to admit he hadn't asked their last name. His mother and father looked at each other over their coffee cups.

That night when he climbed up into the top bunkbed Henry wondered how he got into such a mess—everyone was sorry for him and he wasn't at all sorry for himself. His legs ached. He lay listening to the night noises coming up from the street. He lay listening to the hum of other people talking on the other sides of walls, behind closed doors. The people on the third floor next door weren't asleep. Squares of light glowed from their windows. Maybe Cocoa had her head tucked under her wing.

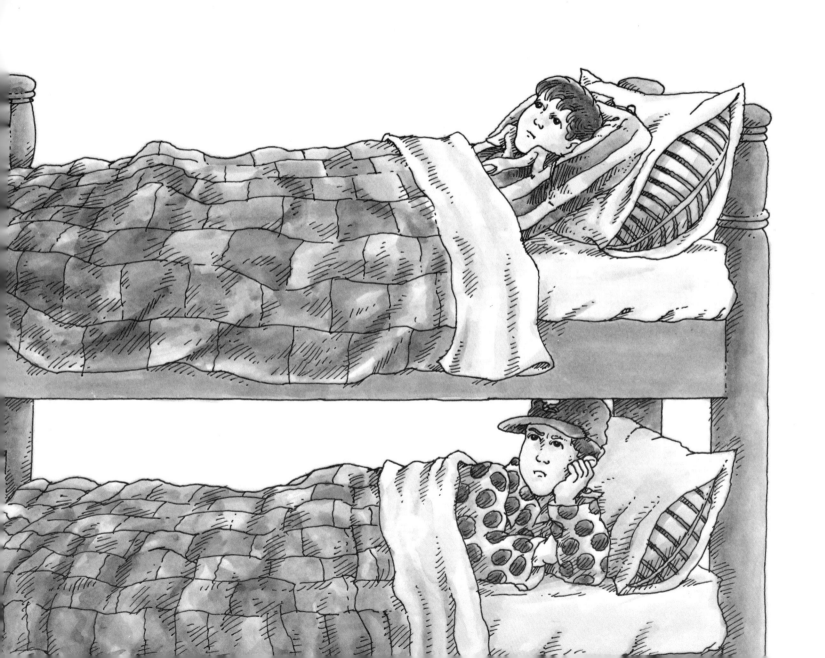

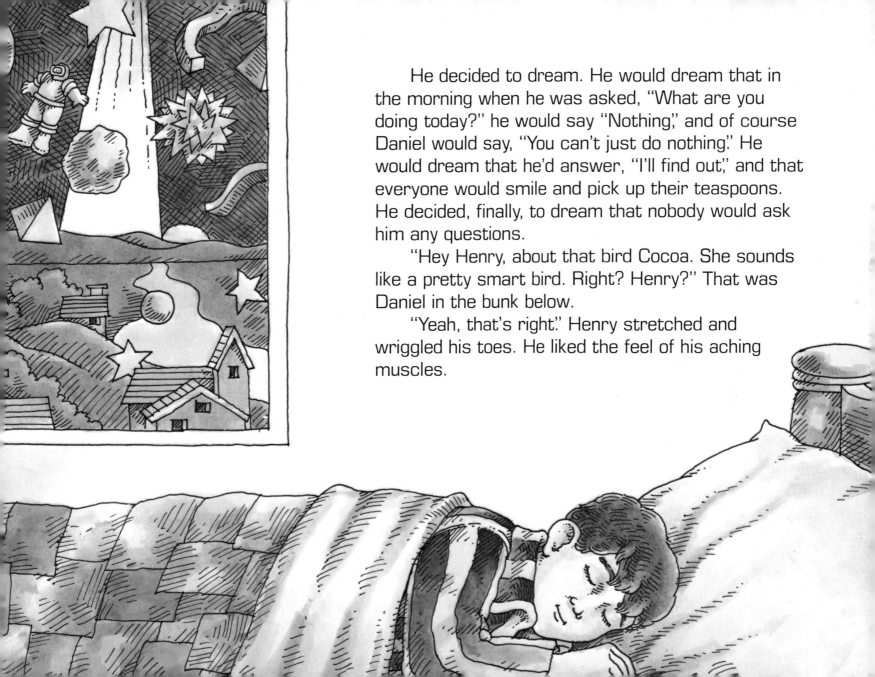

He decided to dream. He would dream that in the morning when he was asked, "What are you doing today?" he would say "Nothing," and of course Daniel would say, "You can't just do nothing." He would dream that he'd answer, "I'll find out," and that everyone would smile and pick up their teaspoons. He decided, finally, to dream that nobody would ask him any questions.

"Hey Henry, about that bird Cocoa. She sounds like a pretty smart bird. Right? Henry?" That was Daniel in the bunk below.

"Yeah, that's right." Henry stretched and wriggled his toes. He liked the feel of his aching muscles.

Maybe Daniel wasn't so bad after all, Henry
thought. It was better to share a room with someone
who wasn't so bad after all. Than with anyone else.

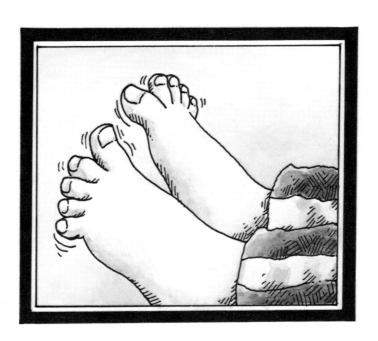

Library of Congress Cataloging in Publication Data

Norris, Louanne, date
"What are you doing today, Henry?"

SUMMARY: Henry begins and ends his day by wiggling
his toes, taking life as it comes in between.
    I. Ross, Larry, 1943-     ill. II. Title.
PZ7.N7925Wh     [E]     74-23492
ISBN 0-07-047252-1